GONE

THE STORY OF A MISSING WOMAN

MICHAEL UCHELLA

ISBN: 9798366960908

DEDICATION

This book is dedicated to all story tellers and story lovers who have not found or have just found my content.

CONTENTS

AWAKE

I woke up startled.

What is going on? I look to my side, I see an old man laying beside me. Wow! Did i really have sex with a sugar daddy? Damn! I left the bed, so his wife wouldn't meet me here and go violent. I looked for my clothes but couldn't find them. I enter the toilet to freshen up. I look in the mirror.

I screamed.

Looking back at me was not me. It was an old me.
Me plus 30 years.
I look like I'm 50 +.

The last thing I remembered was partying hard on December 1st 2022 with my friends. Which was yesterday night.. wasn't it?

What's today's date? Please. Help me.

I screamed even louder. The man on the bed woke up and came to the toilet. 'Awww baby'. He said with a comforting smile. I'm sorry, who're you and who's your baby? What's today's date? Last thing I remember was yesterday night; I went to a pre Christmas birthday party with my friends.

What's going on?' I screamed. Baby, I'm your husband. We've been married for 25 years now. You had an accident last year and it makes it hard for you to remember recent memories and memories immediately after your youth'. He smiled again, comforting. No! This can't be!

Where did all the years go? Who's this strange old man telling me this? 'Where's my mum, sister, family? I remember having a family.
Where are they?' I screamed and wailed. The man looked like he's used to such behavior from me. He didn't seem disturbed.

You were with your whole family during the accident. Everyone died except you. You sustained a severe concussion and you were in a coma for 6 months. You woke up not long ago and since then, you have memory lapses.

Sometimes you don't remember anything from when you're 20 years old, sometimes, you remember everything. Sometimes you don't remember your childhood. All the doctors said you'll get better and we've been going for treatment.

He smiled at me. I felt absolutely lost and misplaced. He brought out pictures. I saw pictures over the years.

Unfortunately I still can't remember anything at all. God. I feel so lost and confused.

'What's today's date?' I asked him fearfully.

'It's December 1st 2022' he said with a smile. 'What?!' Am I caught in a time loop? What's happening? Who's this man?

I fainted.

DON'T TRUST

I woke up on the bed. Your name is Lena, the strange man who called himself my husband said. Suddenly I had a flashback. It was my friends and i going out and so happy, young and free. 'We got married in 1997. Do you remember anything from then?' He said. I tried to, but nothing came forth. This is tough. My life is a wisp. How can I not remember?

Something vibrated near me and I jumped. It was a metal looking box. What is this? As if sensing my question, he smiled again. 'This is your phone, It's a device for communication'. I looked at the strange box. Phones? The last I remember of such contraptions was the long cord phones.

I remember twining them around my hands whenever I visited my friends house to call a man called Emma. 'Are you Emma?' I asked. I saw his face tighten a bit before releasing. 'No dear, I'm Lanre.' Lanre? How come his name isn't even sparking any memories? I picked up the phone and suddenly, I just knew how to operate it.

I went straight to photos and sure enough, there's tons of photos with me and Lanre on the phone. Maybe he truly is my husband. I felt calmer. 'I have to go to work now, don't worry; watch the videos on your phone, we normally do a video diary for you to keep track of your life and the missing bits and pieces' he smiled warmly.

I said okay and started watching the videos. Slowly, my questions started getting answered. After some time, I went downstairs and I saw that he's written something on a sticky note. 'Cook Amala, gbegiri and ewedu. Ingredients in the pantry. Do the laundry, the machine is in the first bath by your right. I love you Lena. Kisses'.

This felt familiar, I sighed. From the video Diary, I learned that I can't keep a job due to my kind of Amnesia, Lanre is a rich executive in a Fintech organization, we don't have maids, housekeepers or anybody living with us because I panic whenever I see strangers (I forget everything). We have 2 children who're in Australia. I felt compassion fill me at Lanre.

I can't imagine what he has to go through daily by reminding an amnesiac wife about everything. I wonder how my situation is affecting him. I feel so bad. I feel worse for myself because the last thing I remember today is Dec 1st 1996 when I went to a party with my friends. It's exactly 26 years later. What does this mean?

Something hovers at the back of my mind but I can't pinpoint it. I unconsciously went to the note part of my phone that unlocked with my face.

The first thing I saw was 'Don't trust Lanre'. All my initial fears came rushing back.

I started reading.

SUSPICION

As I started reading the diary, I heard the horn of a car and I had to stop. 'Don't trust Lanre' just kept ringing in my head. Why would I write that about my 'husband'. I quickly wrote down everything that happened today in my notes, then I heard Lanre walk in.

He came straight to kiss my forehead. I felt nothing. 'Do I ever remember you?' I blurted. 'No' he said sadly. Wow. I can't imagine how that makes him feel. He got ready for bed and tried to touch me. I looked at him confused. 'I'm sorry, I'm not in the mood,' I whispered. I could sense his dissatisfaction.

But I'm not about to allow a man I know nothing about to touch me. Immediately he slept off, I picked up my phone and went back to the notes. Why shouldn't I trust Lanre?

I kept on reading. I was desperate to know because I'm sure that once I wake up tomorrow, I will start afresh again. Also, I have to write this down. I got to a part of the note that mentioned a woman called Ade. Suddenly my memory sparked.

I could see Ade so clearly. She loves wearing braids. She's gorgeous and she's my best friend. So, why is it that I can't remember anything about Lanre? His name should spark something isn't it? I got to my last entry in my note (yesterday). Here's what it said:

30th November 2022:
You have to contact Ade by all means. She has the key. She will tell you everything. Never ask Lanre about Ade.

It began to make a little sense. Apparently I've been suspecting something and I've been carrying out my own little investigation on the side, and now I have to figure out who Ade is without Lanres help. I decided to write my progress down:

1st Dec 2022,

You wasted all day trying to figure out who you are! You don't have the luxury of time. Tomorrow, stop asking unnecessary questions. Figure out who Ade is and get to work!

After writing this, I had to set a notification alarm so that I could remember to check my notes. I went to my Contacts on my phone, I can only see Lanres' contact. It's empty. I'm so confused. How do I find Ade now? It's clear to me though that Ade is a major piece in my amnesia. I put my phone down and tapped lanre.

He woke up. 'Can I speak to our children?' I said. 'No, they're hurt seeing you like this because you always forget them', He said. What? No matter what, why won't my kids want to hear from me? All these stories are not adding up. He went back to sleep and I quickly added extra notes about Lanre into my diary. Tomorrow, I must figure it out!

HOME AT LAST (FINAL)

I woke up confused. Where am I? Who's this man lying beside me? Something buzzed beside me and I saw the box. I picked it up and it was a reminder. I opened my notes and saw the last thing I wrote last night. Ade! Yes. I tried to remember any other thing e.g. Her full name, to no avail. What's going on? I dropped it back and laid on the bed. Who is Ade?

I let calm wash all over me. Slowly, and painstakingly, with sheer will, the memories of Ade started flashing. Holding hands. Attending parties. Hosting a party with a gorgeous man called Emma. Emma. I gasped. He came into full view in my memory. Tall, fine, with a dimpled cheek. My chest ached with familiarity. I picked up my phone and quickly jotted something short about Emma.

I tried to focus on Ade but I could not remember anything. I went to the browser On my phone and typed 'Ade McGuire'. Articles and pictures came up. They fit the woman in my head. Older pictures though. Wow. So, this is Ade. She is a professor and apparently my best friend. I copied her directory and waited for Lanre to leave the house until I made contact.

Before he left, he gave me some drugs to use to improve my memory. Somewhere in my notes, I jotted that I should pretend to use the drugs, so I always threw them away. We made the normal sounds and he was off. I quickly grabbed the phone to call Ade.

Ade McGuire;

Hearing Lena on the phone was like honey to my ears. She sounded so lost! She was babbling, crying and confused. She wasn't even sure if she could trust me; but she kept babbling that her diary (which are notes of everything she remembers daily) asked her to call me. Lena! We have been searching for her for 20 years now.

Since 2002 we have searched for you but found no clues. No bodies, Nothing. At first I was suspicious that it was a pretender, but she is able to answer questions as far back as 1994 when we were in the university. I decided to proceed with caution.

She didn't know her location, so I directed her on how to use WhatsApp and then live location. Turns out she's in Abuja. Luckily, I flew in from Lagos to a conference in Abuja. Without further ado, I enlisted the help of some uniformed Officers and we went to the address. Lena is perfectly safe and sound.

Lanre;

I can't help it. Something is wrong. Have I become too lax? Was it wrong to give her a phone? Have I trusted her too much? Over the years; I've depended on the drugs and her daily memory loss to keep things in order for me. But what's going on? Why do I have this feeling that something is wrong?

Emma;

Losing Lena on Dec 1st 2002 was the most demoralizing thing to ever happen to me. My wife, My love, My baby. We were newly weds, happy to start our life together. She had just started her PhD. We had a little quarrel about something inconsequential and she stormed Off in a fit of anger. She never came back. I could never have closure. I had night mares. I failed her, I failed our kids. Our twin sons keep asking for their mother. I never remarried because I could never forgive myself.

I kept hoping for closure. I went to countless Mortuaries. I went everywhere. I looked for her non-stop for 5 years until the police were tired of my case. I spent all my life fortune on private investigators; but nobody seemed to know where she was. It was like she vanished into thin air. Now, a call from Ade McGuire has ignited my hope. Lena is alive and well? With just some memory loss? Wow! I booked the next flight to Abuja.

Lena;

We didn't spend much time in Abuja. That same day, we left for Lagos with Emma. Ade didn't want to risk 'Lanre' catching us up. I shared the same sentiments. Ade told me everything about my past. My husband Emma and my children; twin boys. They must be adult men now. I've missed so much for the past 20 years. Immediately we got to Lagos, Emma and Ade got me access to the best neurosurgeon in Nigeria. Treatment started.

I met my kids. We cried. Hugged. Loved. It was amazing. I lost so much time. Emma and Ade were hellbent on finding this 'Lanre' who'd kidnapped me for 20 years and bringing

him to justice. Ordinarily, I was okay with that; but I'm scared. I can remember my secret now.
Lanre isn't just anybody, He was my lover. I was cheating on Emma with Lanre.

After the fight in 2002, I rushed in anger to Lanres house to get some angry fucks to cool off. After sex, I wanted to leave, but Lanre started crying & begging, asking me to marry him. I told him I have a husband with 2 kids, this was just for fun. That was the last thing I remembered. After a few more months of therapy, the memories with Lanre started trickling in.

The beatings, the abortions, the hard drugs, the travels, the night life. Lanre beat me and bashed my head against the floor until I bled out. He rushed me to the hospital and after recovery, I lost my memory.

Once I wake up, it's back to that party on Dec 1st 1995 with my friends and now I know why I was fixated on that date. It was at that party I met Lanre.

The end.

ABOUT THE AUTHOR

Michael Uchella is a story writer/teller. He has written several other books and is dedicated to writing stories that help you relax your mind and enjoy reading.